Poems for Guyana's Youth

Haimnauth Ramkirath

New Sunrise Press—Bayonne, NJ
Paperback ISBN: 978-1-7363733-4-7
Hardcover ISBN: 978-1-7363733-5-4
eBook ISBN: 978-1-7363733-6-1
Library of Congress Control Number: 2024910568
Title: *Poems For Guyana's Youth*
Author: Haimnauth Ramkirath
Digital distribution | 2024
Hardcover | 2024
Paperback | 2024

This is a work of fiction. The characters, names, incidents, places, and dialogue are products of the author's imagination, and are not to be construed as real.

Published in the United States by New Book Authors Publishing

Dedication

To the memory of my brother,
Simon Ramkirath

What every child wants is always
in the distance; like the sea
on the horizon. While on the shore
nearby, at the feet of every child
shallow water, eating the edges
of islands and continents does little more,
little more than foam like spittle
at the corners of the inarticulate mouth
of some other child who wants to run
into the sea, into the horizon.

-Martin Carter

Foreword

Who dares write for young people!
Writing in itself is challenging. But writing for youths!
Well, in his new collection, Haimnauth Ramkirath has undertaken this with a beauty that hides the skill, perspiration and endless hours it took in curating his thoughts with exacting use of language to make for easy absorption and digestion.

Of course, you will still see the scars, the healed scars of growing pains, but now worn like medals, badges of honour. And, of course, you will feel and empathize with the author's nostalgia, the longing for bygone (boy-gone) days. The recognition that we have lost something that William Wordsworth intimated in "The World is too much with us....Little we see in Nature that is ours." We cannot help but to reflect if it's not the same sentiment that is echoed in these lines of Haimnauth's:

But now I wonder what has gone—
the gladsome rain holds no charm.
I run and run from every drizzle along the dam.

Something I lost along these pebbled streets and thoroughfares.

It is useful to note that this collection does not start with the author's words but with the words of Guyana's most influential and illustrious poet, Martin Wilde Carter, setting the tone of the collection. With the use of this poem by Carter 'A child ran into the sea,' Ramkirath indicates that he is grounded in the literature of Guyana, the nuances that only literature can bring forth. And he measures up quite admirably alongside his literary ancestors.

To Ramkirath's credit, with this collection, he has added to a short list of Guyanese writing for young people which includes John Agard, Grace Nichols, among others.

I was attracted to Ramkirath's work via social media mainly through the comments to his posts on FB, not so much the likes (from acquaintances) but the connections he made. Connectivity is vital in this sort of lone wolf task of writing, and more so writing for the young, even though writing has its own inherent rewards. Find examples in these poems 'A tap in the shoulders,' 'At the street corner' that is 'stage for every debate and fight,' and 'A felt closeness'…

Not from that little smart ubiquitous thing that knows no rest,
and brings the whole world into the living room or the conference—
but people talking to people in a felt closeness
of a tap on shoulder, a look into the eyes, and a warm embrace.

Something lost when a distance intervenes.
We talk by holding or looking into a screen.

…. The touch of a warm hand—
more than words can ever say,

So, what can we expect in this work – more than meets the eyes. For instance, in his opening poem 'My Young Friends,' he shows two stages of life (it is useful to note here that the collection is divided into two parts):

The world hesitates, but you never doubt
your little hands can send the ball to kiss the clouds.
It's the rope and not your feet that asks for rest—
from the skipping, …

And I would rather be with you for a jaunty while,
than in this place where people grope and whine.
But the knees protest and so does the back,

And he follows up with the stages between, exhorting us to 'listen to stories of your ancestors' as we 'Sway to the beat of the bongo, dolak, and tassa,' describing the festivals of his native land, its folklore, the fauna and flora that come alive in his hand, even the people – workers of the land – are unforgettable like the cow minder, the wood seller, the channa man, the cane cutter, and of course there is cricket, and 'a bottle of rum' – the rum culture.

Ramkirath invokes the wisdom of the grandmother:

"one ounce of prevention better than a pound of cure.
don't hang your hat where your hand cannot reach.
you never miss the water till the well run dry.
what sweet ah goat mouth does sour he backside.
easy snake does bite hot.
moon ah run till day ketch am.
can't suck cane and blow whistle.
every skin teeth is no laugh.
na tek yuh mattee eye fuh see.
what you see daytime, don't look fuh at night with fire stick."

Repeatedly he glorifies the land of his birth. He extols the Kiskadee, the Hibiscus, the grandeur of Kaieteur, the Victoria Amazonica Lily, Laura, the parrot, and the 'Sweet Rain.' He looks past locations reaching to the earth, the naked ground, the pasture, and invoking Cuffy, Kowsilla, the Enmore Martyrs and other freedom fighters as he himself sought to defend the land against Venezuela's Maduro.

Ramkirath knows what education can do, but cautions us while reaching for the stars, to be still grounded. He devotes lots of attention to education, book learning, even as he extols the virtues of nature as the best educator.

A Treasured thing

Hold the book; open it.
Run your fingers along its spine.
Turn the pages and feel them.

Take in that whiff of fresh ink on crisp paper.
It's the best perfume.
It will enter your soul, and be there when you're old.

A good book—a treasured thing.

Here's another treasured thing – nature:

There's no obituary for the fallen saman tree.
No solemn march; no black ribbons worn.
There're no candles; no scribbled messages at its roots.
Not even a mark to show where it stood.

It would be useful to us all as grownups to remember that we have inherited the earth and all wherein – the joys and sorrows etc., and it behooves us that we leave this earth/world in a better state for our descendants to inherit. And Ramkirath exhorts us that in the quest for economic progress, we have to be mindful of what we leave to posterity:

And what a poverty in that prosperity—
clouds leaving a glum trail over thoroughfares and high rises—
when we hear no bees buzzing on the silk cotton tree,
and no frogs croaking in swollen ponds by the deserted churchyard.

Looking back can be heart wrenching but in the hands of a superior storyteller it can be healing and this is what Ramkirath has done in this collection – offer a balance view/perspective of life; this is a gift to young people.

Haimnauth Ramkirath was an educator before migrating to the US in 1991. Haimnauth has published five works of poetry: *At Ease Like the Blooming Lotus, Troubled World, Rhythms of Ease & Wonder, Unsung Verses*, and *Stirrings of Hope & Other Poems*. This is his sixth work showing the development of a writer with much more to share.

Petamber Persaud
Author of 'An Introduction to Guyanese Literature.'

Table of Contents

Part One

Experiences and Enduring Impressions

<u>My Young Friends</u>

Your nimble feet hardly seem to touch the ground.
Show the vines what it means to run.
Show the world how to play in the sun.
Then join hands; I want to see you dance in the ring.
The village wants to hear you sing.

The world hesitates, but you never doubt
your hands can send the ball to kiss the clouds.
It's the rope and not your feet that asks for rest—
from the skipping, skipping, skipping that sends the mind reeling.
The wind wants to play but for that blessed curse to keep moving.

And I would rather be with you for a jaunty while
than where people grope and whine.
But the knees protest, and so does the back,
and this giddy world would not afford me some slack
to play with my young friends on this chalk-smitten track.

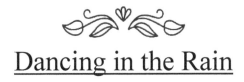

Dancing in the Rain

The batters shouted for every run
when the rain came and flooded the pasture ground.
We danced in the wind-swept rain
with a fun-filled glee not to be contained.

The rain thought it strange we showed such revelry
in the drenching, drenching, drenching in the open.
Every kiskadee, robin, and blue saki found shelter in the jamun trees.
But what's that haven to the playfulness in the pelted rain?
We sang as handfuls of mud splashed on faces and backs.

We jumped into the streams—a sweet rushing as from the tides,
and carried by an urgency we were glad to abide,
but only for a while—we built dams, we arrested the flood,
and with bare hands and mud.

We feared no body ache, chill, or fever.
We floated with a sweetness from the flung rain.
The sun could not wait; it came out to watch the merry show,
and sent us the token of a splendid rainbow.

We courted dark rain-bearing clouds over fields and rugged hills.
But now I wonder what has gone—
the gladsome rain holds no charm.
I run and run from every drizzle along the dam.

Something I lost along these cobbled streets and thoroughfares.
A little aching, but a tender rousing—watching children in the rain.
Then my heart leaps and dances with them—in the wind-swept rain.

Children of the Earth

O ur bare feet knew the grass, mud, and dirt
but not the sleek concrete that hid the face of the Earth.
A sweet sight to behold—
the imprint of little soft feet on the pasture ground.

Heaps of cow dung around,
and the fun when our feet tasted of the filling, half-done.
We knew the stones and pebbles on every dam.
The life of every germ, tadpole, and worm pulsated on our palms.

The sky in every clear pond.
Our hands tried to reach that vaulted blue.
They made the waters murky.
The sky was gone,
but we learned not to trouble the tranquil face of the pond.

I wondered how we remained unscathed
when we ran close to uncouth fearsome things:
wooden planks with rusted nails jutted from their bellies,
umbrella limbs and corroded zinc scattered by the wind,
and bedeviled brooms and broken bottles and beer cans
that waited long in the rain and sun for one last dance.

And if we had any claim to a sweet innocence,
it could only be because we were children of the Earth.

The Fallen Saman Tree

A foul deed brought down the saman tree.
But we hear no cries
and no voices raised at this act of insensate rage.

The wind saw blood on its hands and ran.
But who will apprehend a thing that rides unseen,
and miles afar fetches the fragrance of jasmine.

There's no obituary for the fallen saman tree.
No solemn march and no black ribbons worn.
There are no candles and no scribbled messages at its roots.
Not even a mark to show where it stood.

No one bids farewell to the fallen saman tree.
A thing that stood in beauty;
a thing blotted from memory.

But the wrens, robins, and sparrows stand in a vexed silence.
They gaze long at the fallen saman tree.

They will find another but will long remember
the tree where they sang and darted from limb to limb,
and as fledglings saw the deep blue and broke the raging wind.

They seem to feel the pain when a tree is gone,
and the world never the same.

The Hibiscus

It opens with the freshness of morning raindrops on its face.
It adorns every yard, every fence, and every gate.
It colors our frenzied world; it brightens our days.
Who would begrudge its sprightly ways?

But at high noon, the hibiscus cries for the wind and rain—
not a howling and drenching, but a caring
like a soothing balm for the blisters on its skin.

The hibiscus shrivels and lowers its head,
and from what wrong or regret,
but an animated gaze at the rising sun.

No hands stretching to shield it from the fiery torment.
No respite in the searing stillness of the moment.
When the old man looks at its bruised face and cries,
he decries the Universe for such disdain.

But I hear the drums of thunder; rains are pouring.
Tomorrow, the hibiscus will be smiling.
Tomorrow, the hibiscus will be smiling.

Call of the Kiskadee

C all of the Kiskadee from the tall and elegant mango tree.
A rousing call to open windows and behold
sun-drenched coconut palms swaying in the Atlantic breeze.

The call of kiss-kiss-kiss-kadeeeee in the village in the midday heat,
as the sun scorches every grass and pebble on the pasture ground,
and folks retreat to the shade of the tamarind tree.

The call of the kiskadee resounds when the cows come home,
and in the vanishing traces of untold shades of colors and light—
it pierces the stillness of the twilight—a sweet prelude to the night.

What's in that little heart of the yellow-breasted kiskadee
to sing from morn to night with bursts of high-pitched strings,
dart from limb to limb, and the nerve to break the raging wind?

I wonder if it's the call of the kiskadee that some show such sweetness
in eyes, though poor for want of the necessities of life.

Bansi

Hear the cows mooing in the stillness of dawn,
and Bansi calling them out one by one.
Taking them to graze on the pasture ground
where hills look down on lush grass around.

It's fun to watch Bansi with a stick in hand
urging the cows along and breaking into a song
as the sun hastens to show its face
to see Bansi and the cows and the dust they raise.

Before the sun in its bed of crimson-red to rest,
and the lotus sinks under the murky depths—
Bansi on his wonted lonely trek.
Gathering the cows and calling them out one by one
with a vexed eagerness they seem to understand—
to follow him home and sleep and dream in the comfort of the barn.

At the Street Corner

There were taps on shoulders and fingers pointed at faces.
There were jokes, noise, and outrageous laughter.
And to every story and news—
flair, color, and added layers—when we gathered at the street corner.

The people saw the cricket test match at Bourda
from every vantage point at the street corner.
Every crack of the willow on ball, every fall of wicket,
every catch in the slip, and every dive at the boundary rope.
Every ball that swung and turned with guile and magic on its face.
They saw when the umpire raised his finger or shook his head
and the quarrel on the field whether the ball was alive or dead.

We carried the fun into the dark.
Auntie Bettie called out to her children, one by one,
for dinner of roti, cabbage curry, and prawns.
The watchman at the water pumping station
shouted for some respite to sleep—his shift had just begun.

We courted bad dogs and pitched darkness at midnight.
But the Milky Way waved its arms in delight.
Some swore they saw Uncle Joe, gone many years ago,
came out of his yard with cutlass, shovel, and hoe.

The street corner—stage for every debate and fight,
but no blows and no bell to save from the rush of blood and bile.
The hot-headed raised their voices, but not their reason,
until the rains drowned the heated argument.

Laura

Laura, my parrot, is a pretty dainty thing.
She talks, laughs, curses, and sings.
I never clipped her wings—
she sits on treetops in the unspoiled, unbounded air,
but ever comes back to stand on my shoulders to stare,
and, as if on a stage, to prattle away in her wonted ways.

She says things not meant for the ears of a child.
I wonder where she got such schooling but without a hint of guile.
She yells at the hot-tempered and moneylenders with crooked tricks.
She's no witness to nefarious deeds on an ill-fated ship.
Laura listens to my tale of woe when I am in despair;
I could tell she cared.

Laura screams at every cherry and mango, not to her taste,
and at everyone who enters the yard with a sour face.
She riles at the old lady who fetches news of every affair
and laughs when she slips and falls on the slippery stairs.
But she likes the little boy who brings the milk,
and talks to him with words, soft and smooth like the finest silk.

Behold Laura's colors fluttering in the Atlantic wind
when the Golden Arrowhead unfurls as the children sing.
And brilliant and bold, colorful and fancy,
and a hint of time-honored ceremony—
the Amerindians' headwear bedecked with Laura's feathers—
wafted downward to emblazon Earth.

Childhood Days

No concrete hemmed the pasture ground, hills, trenches,
and dusty pathways of our childhood days.
We hugged the Earth; we basked in every sunrise.
We knew every patch of the soft, dew-laden grass.

The sun hardened layers of mud on our feet
and (with a stern look) healed bruises on knees.
We wished it had watched our play—
a sweet delay to prolong the day.

We bemoaned fading days; we hated shades of gray.
But when the rains came in torrential downpours,
we sent our little Pinta, Nina, and Santa Maria to exotic shores.

The song of the kiskadee regaled our sun-drenched days.
Tadpoles in the pond were a string of black pearls.
We scouted for ripened 'monkey apples' along the mudflats.
We poked our fingers into the holes of bundarie crabs.

We watched fields of cane on fire—crackling noise, flying ash,
and reddish flames that leaped and devoured the leafy trash.
And when the show was over, we scampered for the best
of joints tied in bundles on slender shoulders.

What fun when the star-pointed diamond kite mounted,
sang and danced, and brushed its tail on the lush Earth.
But when it dashed into a guava tree—its forlorn face—
the first note of sadness in our childhood days.

The Masquerade Band

Fifes, flutes, fiddles, kettle and boom drums, and shac-shac—
festive music and beats of the masquerade band along the street.
Children ran to see the fun.
Every man and woman frolicking in sweet music.
There was much dancing, wining, and flouncing,
and revelers moving and grooving on Christmas morning.

Costumes—a patchwork of outlandish colors.
A mismatch never seen;
more bizarre with the ghoulish masks.
Men danced on stilts.
"Long Lady" brushed the clouds away;
it was a sun-drenched day.
Mother Sally gyrated with a big, big behind.
There was much dancing, wining, and flouncing,
and revelers moving and grooving on Christmas morning

Nani and Nana pranced and danced by the gate,
and incited the band to raise the music like Jouvay on Christmas day.
Big Bertha brought out black cake and mauby.
Every reveler on the street had a treat.
There was much dancing, wining, and flouncing,
and revelers moving and grooving on Christmas morning

Then the music stopped,
The leader of the band raised his voice.
Revelers and onlookers listened to every word:
"Christmas comes once a year,
and every man shall have his share,
but poor brother Billie in jail
drinking sour ginger beer! Blow! Blow!"
Fifes, flutes, fiddles, kettle and boom drums,

triangle and shac-shac heeded the leader's call.
The verve and energy flooded the street.
There was much dancing, wining, and flouncing,
and revelers moving and grooving on Christmas morning.

And the man with the "Bull-Cow" rushed to the crowd.
Children saw the lowered horns.
They saw fire in the bull's eyes.
They ran; they came back—
a dangerous thing to tease a mad bull born to gore.
But what a spectacle:
the sweet mischief of children and bull.
There was much dancing, wining, and flouncing,
and revelers moving and grooving on Christmas morning.

Black Sage, Coconut, and Castor Oil

I pounded the end of the black sage—
the best bristles ever made.
They needed no Colgate.
They made my teeth whiter than the feathers of the Snowy Egret.

I rubbed coconut oil on my head and body.
When I parted the hair, the fine-toothed comb drenched by oil.
The good oil shone on every page of my writing books.
Every word and number dripped in coconut oil.
And when I came out to play,
such sheen on a dark skin never seen by sun and wind.

The imprint of coconut oil on everything I touched.
To think I was the poster child of the Earth.
And everywhere I went, the wind fetched the scent
of coconut oil, far and wide over fields and trenches.

And I drank, after a little coaxing, the dreaded castor oil.
I pitched a tent close to the latrine.
And all day I became a standpipe—
a trickle, a burst, then a stoppage,
as was the nature of standpipes in those days.

The neighbor startled at the sprint from tent to latrine.
But, sweet relief from the chicken broth
that brought to the pipe the murmur of a froth.

Leaks and Potholes

When it rained in the day or night,
we heard the unwelcomed sound of drip, drip, drip
in every room, the hallway, and kitchen.
Not one that sent us to sleep,
but to scurry for every bowl, saucepan, and plastic bucket
until the house was a festival of drums but with a steady beat.

Every pothole on every road smiled
with ripples like those of a lake.
When I came from the late-night show,
I wished my boots had sensors
to point them out in the pitched darkness.
I slipped into the muddied waters in every pothole.
The boys taunted me for not knowing the ways of the road.

During the day, I stayed far from those potholes.
But it got me mad when the taxi drivers
came too close to wash their wheels.
They drenched me from head to heels.
I ran after them with a volley of curses.
I called out for a fight, fist to fist.
But those taxi drivers could not contain their wits,
and drenched me again on the return trip.

High Tide in the Woods

It was high tide.
The full moon goaded the waters to frenzied delight.
We heard the thunder at every lash to the battered wall.
The bruised timbers of the sluice shook.
The tide rushed into the woods.

The bisi bisi and moco moco bush steadied their heads
though their knees in waters deep.
The crabs would rather sleep than wait for the tide to recede,
when their ungainly march brought comic relief to the mudflat.

Where to look for the dam and the hill,
the sprawling root and the bump in the woods,
when all covered in raging waters?
But the kiskadee gazed at the sunset with wings outstretched.

We grabbed onto a wooden plank above a narrow, deep pond.
And though we had no ticket to show,
the raging current hurtled us on its train for a boisterous, sweet ride;
a playfulness never seen with such a beating from the tide.

Sweet Rain

Come, sweet Rain.
  Beat down on roof and windowpane
  with streaking rivulets that we know you're around,
and riding on the shoulders of the wind
to spread cherry blossoms on the sacred ground.

Come, sweet Rain.
Wake up every clogged drain, lease water trench, pond, and lake
to look at your gleeful face,
and rejoice in your bounty that makes them overflow
with the gladness in every drop you throw.

Come, sweet Rain.
You bring the magic spell
for chameli, oleander, and bougainvillea to bloom so swell.
The banana leaves know your friskiness—
send you down like from sieves, a little gentler to the ground.

Come, sweet Rain.
The ferocious jaguar runs for cover from your steady showers.
But see the glee on the face of every tree and wildflower.
And that little heart of the kiskadee would have no rest,
if not for your playfulness that makes this land blessed.

The Kite

The mounted star-pointed kite danced and sang,
but not with the freedom of the Peregrine Falcon
tied to no human hand.

The elated kite ascended higher and higher; it kissed the clouds,
but remembered the pasture ground from whence it came,
and in loops of effervescent delight,
brushed its tail against the lush earth.

The charm and glee in tinseled paper, eta broom, slices of bamboo
skin, gamma cherry, and a ball of braided nylon twine.
When the wind held its breath,
we ran with twine and jumped over pond and ditch,
and all for the kite to lift.
It saw our edginess, then our gladness—it gazed with a steady face
like an ornament held high—a blithe ribbon blazoned against the sky.

But when the wind rushed with an unabated breath,
the kite brushed aside decorum.
It danced with a lusty abandon—
a recklessness that courted razor-wire fences,
high tension power lines stretched over villages,
and boisterous, sprawling rivers and trenches.

That dreaded thrill when it dashed against a tall coconut tree.
The branches caught the frisky limbs of a daring spirit.
They muzzled its song;
drained its heart of every dance.
And we watched a thing born to be free—
stuck on a tree.

Bad Dogs

I was scared of those bad dogs,
more than any Jumbie, Moon-Gazer, Baccoo, or Fire Rass.

They knew no warm, tender touch
or the thrill of running for a ball or a branch tossed in the mud.
They felt no brushes or clipper blades on their skin.
They were hungry, lean, and mean.

They barked, barked and barked at night and in the day
at anyone who passed along the way.
No leash on their neck;
no one yelled to keep them in check.
No scolding for them to stand on one leg.

I clenched no fist and pelted no bricks,
but something in me made those bad dogs crazy.
They seemed to know when I turned the corner;
they rushed at me with eyes of fire.

But I learned not to retreat.
I stared at them like a panther prowling in the jungle deep.
They were as much afraid of me as I was of them.
And a truce declared between bad dogs and boy.

Emboldened, they broke the truce at night.
But I stamped my feet and raised a wallaba stick,
and those bad dogs scampered and growled along the deserted street

Oh! Little Canary

No court sat in hushed silence;
no jury handed a verdict;
no judge pronounced a sentence.

Oh! little canary, how cruel a fate—
imprisoned in a cage,
and for what ill deed—
to sing in the woods, melodies sweet,
kiss the clouds, and roam over waters deep.

Strains of irrepressible melodies from that wretched cage—
never heard in the woods or when you flitted along the rooftop.
The plaintive cry of a spirit removed from its native space,
and only in dreams to behold the sun's face.

If such a fate to any human—shouts of outrage over the land.
But the world in silence conspires to mock your wings and feathers.
Every piece of wood and wire tempered in fire,
and the hardness of a heart that framed a cage
to suppress a spirit that rode over paddy fields
and sat on jamun treetops—its mate to serenade

Blackout

Another night—another blackout.
The curses and shouts as the music stopped,
and Uncle Charlie lumbered for his cloak and cap.
Some took a nap; some talked of load-shedding.
But, by a thousand other names, it didn't assuage the suffering.

We slipped and fell, feeling for the wall.
The frantic search for candles—
they hid their faces in the dark.
Every squash and tilapia curry overcooked and burned.
Old Seenauth knew not which way to turn.
A long centipede crawled into my underpants;
I felt the sting of sitting on a nest of fat red ants.

Flies and mosquitoes mingled in dhal and rice.
We could not push the bones of the gilbaka aside.
And that thick red stuff in the cup of water—
we drank it with every bitter pill we swallowed.

But in the blackout, every hammock—a bed for romance.
Some loved the dying flame of the jug-jug lamp.
We heard the moans and panting for breath
in the sweet silence of the darkness.

Rows of Little Earthen Lamps

W e gathered the fresh earth.
We made little earthen lamps.
They hardened in the sun.
But what softness in heart
to reveal a steady brightness amid encroaching darkness.

Diwali night—every little light awakened to show its might.
Rows of earthen lamps on every step, doorway, and window sill.
When the wind stood still, they smiled and rose with defiance
to smite the primordial darkness over villages, plains, and hills.

I felt the loss when one died in a blustery blast.
But when in the throes of suffocation,
the little earthen lamp emerged with a brightness not seen before—
it brought the gladness of a blithesome face to a distraught world.

Where's the inbred darkness when little lamps invade the cave?
When they glitter in rows along every step we take—
there's no feeling for a way in the pitched darkness.

They Lived in Logies

Folks still talk about life in the logies.
Bitter-sweet memories of no wooden floors or carpets,
but the scent of cow dung plastered on the damp ground.
There was no kitchen faucet to open or close
but a lone standpipe for the neighborhood,
and a brotherhood and sisterhood we little know.

People washed their clothes in the trenches.
There was no Colgate and toothbrush but black sage.
No fashion or style, but simple cotton wear and a smile.
There were no fences or gates, but a shared ground
to play the bongo, dolak, and tassa drums
as they recited the sacred lore of their native land,
and regaled in festive music and dance—
a forgetfulness of the oppressor's cruel heart and hands.

They knew the Earth and the sun-drenched grass,
but dreamt of their children plucking the stars.
For them, they braved the ocean's wrath and the winds' blast.
For them, they toiled in the shadow of the taskmaster's gaze
and moistened those green fields of cane with rivulets of tears.

They heard the virulent knocks of wretched visitors:
dreaded cholera, dysentery, and dengue fever.
And when they ventured from their cramped quarters,
they gazed in awe at the white mansions of the taskmasters;
a world apart—bitter-sweet sugar had wrought.

Earthen Fireside

The dhal cooking—no hissing of steam from a pressure cooker,
but boiling, boiling, boiling in a pot on an earthen fireside.
Baigan and plantain—not wrapped in aluminum sheeting,
but roasting, roasting—softening from inside—in the fireside.

There's no hastening of the cooking,
but a slowing, a chastening from earth, water, fire, and wind
that gives every gilbaka curry, every metemgee, every fever-grass tea
a special taste and flavor when over an earthen fireside.

No gas line, no knobs to turn on or off, or raised to high or low.
A gentle fire from the sticks of the wallaba,
and when choked and giddy with all that smoke—
comes to life with a blowing from the mouth of the pooknee.

When the fireside in the open on the cow dung-smeared ground,
it's easy for peppers on the tree to find their way in a pot of duck curry.
But the earthen fireside needs watchful eyes,
lest there's any overreaching in the play of earth, water, fire, and wind.

And long after we have eaten, the earthen fireside keeps smoldering,
but not like the fire in the belly that blazes to nourish mind and body.

Jug or Kerosene Lamp

W e held the jug or kerosene lamp.
It pointed at the little frog that jumped into the water tank,
It allayed our fears of a jumbie knocking on the door,
when the branch of the mango tree brushed on the window.

It showed the centipede that crawled along the girl's leg,
and then fell and scurred into a pile of bricks
from a licking from the wallaba stick.

And when we ate late at night,
the inviting smile from the jug or kerosene lamp
glanced at flies and mosquitoes on the rice,
the little mouse that nibbled at the roti,
and revealed the bone of the gilbaka fish stuck in the throat.

We trimmed the wick of the jug or kerosene lamp,
lest the light died from an unprovoked annoyance.
We watched its changing moods—
a steady gaze and then a dance
incited by a lively breeze from the Atlantic.
It told us in its wonted ways what it meant to fight the darkness.

Now, fancy lights strung on all the gates.
We grope, stumble, and fall in the flooded daze,
and I wonder if it's because we see no homely smile on the face
of a simple jug or kerosene lamp.

On the Horse Cart

Forget the inviting scent of the posh leather seat
and the soft headrest that lulls you to sleep.
Ride in the open on a horse-drawn cart;
smile at every passerby with a song in the heart.

See how the sun traverses the heavens.
Look at freshly-dug earth, bees, butterflies, and wriggling worms.
Rejoice with every blade of grass dancing in the wind.
Trot, trot, trot—the beat to every song you sing.

You're not alone.
There are wallaba posts to lean on and tar to patch the boats.
The horse knows the rivers on the road
and needs no headlights—stars point the way at night.

What if every car, van, truck, or bus passes you with disdain?
Let them rush and miss the blue saki singing on the sapodilla tree.
What trip can boast of that measured thrill
and sweet diversion in the smell of tar, fresh horse dung, and urine?

The Morning Train

A time when we waited and waited for the morning train.
We talked and laughed and kept a watch for those bright eyes;
to hear the rhythmic chugging along fields of rice.
An ungainly thing—green-coated steel and iron—
but what a steady rocking speed on the slender rails.

All that burly metal tamed when the station master waved the flag.
A forlorn call from the whistles; the brakes hissed and screeched.
The train stopped; out came big blocks of ice
that the portly man at the shop carried on his back.
A fair exchange when the station master and conductor traded flags,
and the train moved as rails cringed with the familiar clickety-clack.

The clipping of tickets before we had time to take a seat.
Schoolgirls chatted and giggled as the train rattled along the tracks.
Some took an early nap; some talked of the Bourda cricket match.
There were arguments and a fight or two, but the train never detained,
and many kept their time on the sound of the morning train.

We saw cane fields, canals and trenches, farmlands and grassy plains
where horses roamed, and crows tore into a donkey's entrails.
We saw pink lilies as they swayed in the morning breeze,
and bamboo trees, moco-moco bush, and nests of killer bees
—all for a ticket to a trip on the morning train.

Now, no sound of the morning or the late-night train,
but the mad rumbling of mini-buses and loud noises from boom boxes.
There's no time to listen to a fellow traveler breaking into a song.
But folks still talk of the fun along those rails leveled and gone
and the conductors who clipped the tickets on the morning train.

To Outrun the Sun

G aze at the spider's web sparkling in the sunshine—
a constellation of stars strung on a branch.
Look at the robin's nest on the fork of a tree—
too delicate a basket for human hands to weave.

Run after the Monarch Butterfly resting on the gooseberry tree.
Send your little ships to brave the seven seas.
Dance when drenched by the rains,
and let the scent of the sweet earth run in your veins.

Don't be distraught when muddied to the knees.
Look at the river from the top of a tree.
Follow a lively stream in the woods,
and sing in the wind with buttercups and reeds.

Do not be afraid to tumble from a hilltop.
Poke your fingers into the holes of bundarie crabs.
Listen to the Kiskadee and the Blue Saki,
and wait for the gentle Manatee to surface on the rough sea.

And in these things—
more than a sweet childhood,
more than a little fun:
you would have dared to outrun the sun.

Ripened Mangos on the Tree

We pelted the ripened mangoes.
They smiled on branches above the windows.
They did not duck to evade the blows;
not one brick came close to their red-yellowish coat.

We grabbed branches within our slender reach,
and shook them as if to uproot the tree.
But the ripened mangoes laughed at our folly
that dared to bring them down by shaking from below.

We prodded at their stems with long bamboo sticks.
They pleaded for no bruises, no unwarranted licks.
Some were caught before they blessed the ground—
the glee greater than any treasure found.

Some showed a pride and an aloofness
and looked down than mingled with dirt on the ground.
Some hid in bloated drains,
but no sweetness wasted, though mud-stained.

But sweetest of all—
those that fell of their own accord,
and laid like ambrosia before the eyes.

Fences

Wished there were no fences—no staves to unsettle
as we moved from yard to yard in our merry, playful ways.
It would have spared me the guilt when I eyed the fullness
of the soursop and the ripeness of its breast.

I waited night after night.
When the gleeful moon pointed out the tempting fruit,
I leaned over the neighbor's fence and picked the soursop.

I cursed every fence and every wall that kept my little hands
from reaching faint reddish cherries and yellowish golden apples.
But then I thought of lovers at the fence,
and the smiling and courting and the amorous jollity restrained—
the fence stamped its feet like a sentinel of the night.

And I wondered what human rage would do
if not checked by a fence or two.
I watched neighbors leaning over the fences.
I saw the venom in their eyes,
and heard curses and things not meant for a child.
The prancing, raising of petticoats, drumming on pots, dancing
and taunting brought more than light relief to those around.

I saw raised fists, and fingers pointed to eyes—readiness for a fight.
A menacing rehearsal, but no nerve for a show.
They never came to blows.
Then, I knew the value of fences.

The School Bell

The morning school bell rang.
It drowned every one of my gushing songs,
the sun-drenched fields, and coconut palms that gently danced.
As the Kiskadee sang on the star apple tree,
I dawdled with reluctant steps in that long line of conformity.

But the same bell, sweet when it sent us out to play—
when it declared the end of the school day.
My little heart showed glimpses of what it couldn't contain—
I climbed every hill, kissed every blade of grass,
and somersaulted beyond the churchyard.

A sordid thing to gaze at a glum, unfeeling blackboard,
and then to feel the sting of wild cane on shoulder
when my eyes sought relief looking at a flock of wandering sheep.

And I wondered then, as I still do now,
what sweet learning can ever spring from a wretched face,
and a hairy hand that wielded the cane with such glee and disdain.

Tiger, the Wood Seller

The people of the village called him Tiger—
the tall, burly wood seller on a horse cart laden with wallaba.
And it was not a clap of thunder,
but the voice of Tiger along the dusty street at the corner.

His fat, broad belt tightly drawn.
What gentle ways with all that brawn.
Tiger greeted everyone with a prayer and a song
and cuddled every newborn.

He toppled the wood as he held the reins,
but not one wallaba tasted the frothy slime in the drain
or slipped away from the pile in the wind and rain.

When we came out to chop the wood,
we found them not afraid but waiting for the blade.
The chopped wallaba stacked on two sturdy sticks.
A strain to bear when we had little care.
We showed such grit—
we unloaded the chopped wallaba near a heap of bricks.

Gopi, the 'Channa Man'

The aroma of spiced channa wafted over the village.
Bare-footed, we dared the midday fire
as Gopi, the "channa man," turned the corner.
No fuss for a torn shirt or a nudge in the back
in that sweet rush for Gopi's channa.

We munched on the channa in funneled-shaped beige paper.
We forgot that sting of marabunta on shoulder.
We ate every handful with smiles and laughter.
Licked the salt and peppers that adorned our fingers,
and searched and tore the funnel for that lone channa
that hid its face—it was the best of the crispy fare.

That special touch and taste no more on the things we eat.
Look, and you will see not the hands of Gopi
but the arms and blades of a machine that chop, mix, blend,
and throw a neat package on a giddy, long line.
We hear no love song and no greeting as from a gushing spring.
No tapping on the shoulder from one who's like a friend.
There's no scent of wildflowers or any hint of the earth—
we rue the loss in every spoonful of the dessert.

My Cane Cutter Friend

There's no memo to read
or office meeting to drain the hours of the day.
No sitting on a chair upholstered in leather.
No climbing on a ladder.
But a brutal standing and bending,
and cutting the canes in sun, rain, and wind.

My cane cutter friend knows the dusty, beleaguered way
and the stench of clogged trenches.
Steady and strong, his grip on the cutlass.
If the world could see the corns and calluses on his hands;
fissures on his heels that cry for the kiss of an ointment.

He knows the strength of his shoulders, back, and arms,
and what it means to his family and the little house
tucked in the shadow of the hilltop where wildflowers grow,
and raindrops knock on ramshackled windows.

He's up before the fisherman brings in the haul,
and the kiskadee breaks the silence with its first call.
He hums a song as his beaten, rickety bike makes its way
to the backdam before the sun spreads its rays,
and the lotus rises from the muddy pond to behold the dawn.

The blade of the cutlass bends to his every whim.
He wields it with a savagery and grace.
Acres of canes fall flat on their face.
But his work half-done,
though sweat, mixed with dust, floods the ground.

He rests on his head a fat bundle of canes.
Who would not cringe with such strain?

My cane cutter friend runs on a narrow plank
to drop the canes into the punt choked to the rim.
The risk of a slip and a fall in every grueling trip.
But who can defy the slippery mud
like my cane cutter friend who holds no grudge against sun or rain?

And before the sweltering heat of the mid-day sun,
my cane cutter friend on his beaten, rickety bike heading home—
humming a song that tells of his beloved waiting for his eager hug.

In the Cast Net

I t's a tangled mess—the braided nylon twine—
until it's stretched on a long fat line,
and scolded by rain, wind, and sun
to obey the fisherman's commands,
as he stands on a beaten, slimy rock with net in hands.

He gathers the strength of his shoulders, back, and arms,
and throws the net— a short-lived scintillating dance,
and then a lovely pattern as it kisses the dark waters,
and sinks like a wreath of lead.

The fisherman waits and waits and waits.
A felt strain on the cord as he brings in the haul.
It tells of a fierce tussle—
a raw, pitched battle with a big, big Gilbaka
that tears every fiber of my fisherman friend.

Fish and man in a long, fierce fight.
A test of strength like buffaloes locked in horns.
The blood on the moss-infested rocks.
But the slippery fish defies every grab, hook, and lash,
rips the net, and leaves the fisherman aghast, with hands on head.

Old Higue

The old lady, lean and haggard, walked the dusty streets at noon.
Her accustomed ways betrayed not a hint of the evil
the night brought upon her beleaguered face—
an accursed fate to a devilish delight,
and the revolting name of Old Higue.

They said she had no choice but to obey the vile call.
She dropped her skin in a calabash.
She became a ball of fire—
she leaped and flew through the window,
at the creepy hour to beguile sweet infant child—
to pierce its flesh and drain every drop of blood until it was dead.

The ghoulish name followed her on every street and marketplace.
Villagers pointed at her face; children made chalk marks at her gate.
The ropes they made to tie her down, whips for a good licking,
and soot to smear on her face when dragged for a shaming.
But none ever caught her counting, one by one, a bucket of rice,
or changing into her grimy petticoat at night.

And I kept a lookout through the night;
I saw no Old Higue.
Better, if I had looked in the broad daylight
for one not with crooked bones and a broomstick,
but with a suit and silken tie and a bag full of dirty tricks,
and doing the work of the Old Higue before our very eyes.

The Obeah Man

When he walked along the dusty streets,
few dared to look at his bedazzled face,
lest he sent an ill wind to blight their days.
But people came to the Obeah man from near and far-off places,
and at hours that stretched into the night.

He scribbled a prayer on coarse brown paper;
the sick drank it in a cup of water.
He blew away the infant's fever.
All rushed to the Obeah man's gate for every belly ache,
and every devilish thing spiked into a bottle of lemonade.

And they brought to him Uncle Willie when he ran to catch the wind,
and shouted at every wave to stop.
Incense flooded the Obeah man's room; he went into a trance.
He spoke a strange tongue; he banged his head on the floor.
He plucked a strand of hair, bottled it with ungainly care,
and declared he exorcised the demon in Willie's mind.

Neighbors heard lashes and cries—
a dogged fight between Obeah man and evil spirit entrenched.
Some swore they saw how he wrestled the "jumbie,"
grabbed its neck and flung it into the sea.
But the man along the street said he was no more healer
than the farmer, barber, butler, bricklayer, or shoemaker.

In the Cemetery at Night

I lost my way; I saw a faint light.
It led me through a cemetery in the dead of night.
I saw accursed bones and wraithlike faces but with no feet.
I heard the spookish laughter and the gnashing of teeth
in the silence of the wind and the eerie refrain of the leaves.
But not near the forlorn graves or by the cemetery's gates.
There, all calm—a meditation for the sage.

Whence these spectral images, these legions of an incorporeal fate?
They rushed into my mind like loathsome waters into a strait,
and there found that place, that fount of woeful imagination
that confounded my every nerve and limb,
and sent me shaking and sweating with every whisper of the wind.
I could neither shout nor sing,
and though I tried to run as if with wings,
my feet were pillars of lead—
I stood transfixed on the ground of the dead.

With that faint light that beckoned afar,
I drove them out from every corner of my mind and heart
with a fat broom, harsh words and curses, and a bolted door.
They vanished but not like the mist when the sun rises,
but rather like the dreaded cobra the mind begets
from a coiled rope on the ground with one end
flattened and raised to kiss the fading sunset.

Bites and Bumps on Skin

They crowd clogged drains, standing water, unkept yards,
slender grasses, and the belly of every cupboard and closet.
They heed any darkness to puncture flesh and feast on blood.

We slap our faces, legs, hands, backs, and necks to drive them away.
We don't mind the self-inflicted pain; we grab a book, a ruler, a towel,
a slip-on shoe, or a flat piece of wood to give a wallop and warning.
It's a telling blow when one or two stretched on mortuary slab of flesh.
But an untroubled guilt when our very blood smears ruler or hand.

A wretched noise they blared right into our ears.
The daring reconnaissance tells on the nerves.
They mock our rest and sleep with their fiendish noise and bites.
Who would think such little things could make such bumps on skin.
And when one finds its way into the net—
that's when our defense makes the enemy entrenched.

We never give consent for them to draw our blood.
But they thrust six spears into the skin; they suck the precious fluid.
For our forbearing, no 'Thank You' note; no cup of hot chocolate,
but a vial of saliva—it's their way of planting a kiss,
and what a wretched kiss that carries in it:
Chikungunya, Zika, West Nile, Malaria, Dengue and Yellow Fever.

And they can boast with pride and glee on the cherry tree:
the comingling of human blood in their fat belly.

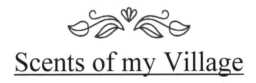

Scents of my Village

The scents and smells of the village I knew.
They rode on the wings of the Atlantic winds.
They left their imprint on my shoulders
long after I passed the limits of their purview.

The scent of fresh earth mixed with twigs and leaves.
The hint of ripeness from mangoes and star apples tucked in raw rice.
The fragrant blast of mint, thyme, and the holy Tulsi
flooded the yard—with stories to tell.

From the corner stand near the school yard,
inviting zest of mauby, mango chutney, bara, and poularie.
And drifting from windows that whiff of delicacy:
cookup rice and metemgee, chicken curry and dhal puri.

Fried breadfruit and sweet potatoes—a tempting trail along the road.
The aroma of fruit cake and corn bread in the oven,
and when I came home from play on the pasture ground,
the pungent air of smoked herring and sliced onions.

The scent of chopped wallaba wood for the fireside,
and cow dung plastered on the ground and left to dry.
In every morning walk—the smell of soft, dew-laden grass,
moss and seaweeds, and beaten trunks of trees stranded on the rocks.

I loitered near the yard where the scent of Jessamine
and Chameli flowers mingled with that of the Oleander,
and a long walk to the backdam for the ethereal fragrance
of the pink lotus rising undefiled from muddy waters.

Grandma's Sayings

When we picked the tempting genip from the neighbor's yard,
and tore our shirts on the fence and slipped and fell,
Grandma's sayings gushed like waters from a well.

It's a different world but Grandma's sayings still ring true,
like the playfulness of the Atlantic and the silence in its depths.

Sometimes like the scent of black sage, thyme, mint, and lavender—
refreshing as if sitting on the summit of Roraima,
and then sometimes like the springing of a leopard—
a hint, a warning lest I be taken by the wily ways of the world.

They still regale my heart and mind like rich red wine,
and who would scorn what Grandma said
while she fed the needle with the long blue thread:

"One ounce of prevention better than a pound of cure
don't hang your hat where your hand cannot reach
you never miss the water till the well run dry
what sweet ah goat mouth does sour he backside
easy snake does bite hot
moon ah run till day ketch am
can't suck cane and blow whistle
every skin teeth is no laugh
na tek yuh mattee eye fuh see
what you see daytime, don't look fuh at night with fire stick."

The Irrepressible Atlantic

She holds a love; she holds a dread,
and both there in her depths.
She soothes; she frightens,
but not with the same breath,
like a traveler telling a story,
with a blending of calmness and violent temper.

I remember when the sun rose from her breast,
and I gazed at the gifted gold on her face.
The waves caressed the sand as in a musical interlude;
pain and strife melted in an unearthly quietude.
A thing too blessed to last.
Before the day had passed,
the convulsive waves battered the shore,
and mighty surges thundered and drenched my soul.

And I beheld those things,
time, water, sun, and wind touched with unbridled wings.
The beaten wall ceded in places.
Timbers covered by barnacles and slime.
Roofs of zinc corroded by the salty mist.
Houses with tales of climbing vines.
Sagging fences in haunted decline.

But that watery realm under the vaulted blue—
the irrepressible Atlantic: untouched by time.

Sunset Over the Essequibo River

I stared at the sun gradually sinking
into the bosom of the mighty Essequibo River.
A fading lamp,
but a thousand delights compressed
in a span of moments—
a blaze on the firmament
as a sublime net with the glow of molten lava
settles over the time-honored river.

A parting gift—
a bed of crimson red the sun makes to rest.
Like blooms of the Royal Poinciana tree scattered on the horizon
and streaming through fabrics of clouds.
The embrace and dance of color and light,
and below the verdant forest alight.

Compelled to gaze long
until that lamp was gone.
Still, ten thousand shades of vanishing light
and sound of the approaching winged chariot of the night.

Among those who know the river,
the old boatman breaks into a song.
Deep silence fell over water and land
Then—
that majestic curtain abruptly closed:
darkness swallows every trace of its eternal foe.

The Jaguar

T he big cat watching with stern eyes.
  Waiting, waiting, and crouching on the plains of the savannah.
  Its tawny yellow coat of black spots and rosettes
belie a meanness and savagery in its breast.

Moving with languid ease;
the tall grasses unruffled by this stealthy beast.
Then, it's a burst of gathering speed
like a winged black stallion breaking gate for the wild wind.

Ground and forest startled by the ferocious leap of the Jaguar,
thrusting its spear-like teeth into the skull of a lone deer or capybara,
stumbling and falling in the throes of a death struggle,
and the Jaguar, ripping it apart with grisly jaws and muscles.

But now the savage beast, hiding, hiding
from that more savage beast in humans
whose strength is the cowardice not to fight with hands, feet, and teeth,
but a rifle mounted on a Land Rover on a far-flung hilltop.
A silken-clad beast of unadulterated cruelty who sees no beauty,
but profits when claws and teeth of the Jaguar sold in exotic markets,

Anaconda

Head above shallow waters along the Kassikaitya River.
The treachery in those big, bulging eyes.
The artistry on its skin glazed with dark olive green
and yellow round brown blotches and a dark stripe.

What in all of nature can smother with that wretched embrace,
when the anaconda's coils of death around a capybara's neck?
No gushing of blood, no protruding gut, no tearing of flesh,
but a constricting that breaks every bone of the capybara's neck
as it convulses in the throes of an agonizing death.

A gluttonous creature that swallows the capybara whole,
and for that, the curse of a hideous belly like a tube overblown,
and a sluggishness the muddy grass knows too well.

A thrill when the old man grabs its neck and steadies its head,
as sturdy lads stretch its body, convoluted in a grisly sleep,
and measure it against a tall, fallen greenheart tree.

Perfume of the Victoria Amazonica

The perfume of the giant Victoria Amazonica Lily
rises above shallow waters of the Amazon;
reaches no thoroughfares of humans—
yet, is not wasted.

Its aroma lingers in tracks of capybaras.
Sits on branches where toucans gather,
and scarce desires the languid air of towns and cities,
and beaten paths of anxious faces.

The perfume of the giant Victoria Amazonica Lily,
like the cloud-drenched peaks of the Pakaraimas,
in self-contented bliss rests,
and cares little if the world be impressed—
a gift so swell to the rainforest.

Like frankincense in the temple,
it rises at the wind's behest,
over insects and frogs in the dark forest—
as waters of the Amazon rise and fall.

Children of Guyana

Children of this sun-drenched land
where the Atlantic rises with mist-laden songs
to gladden coconut trees, crotons, and ferns.
Where the Canje Pheasant muses along the river bank,
and the Harpy Eagle soars above the unspoiled hinterland.

And you, like the Harpy Eagle and the Falcon,
can reach great heights, but not in a sudden flight.
It takes a tireless striving in the fury of the wind,
and the courage to face the disdain of those who mock your daring.

Then it would not be a fanciful thing
to stand at the peak of Roraima smiling,
to pluck a feather of a parrot cutting the air above the rafters,
catch a hummingbird hovering in a wonderous flight,
or snatch that band of red from a stunning rainbow overhead.

But start by knowing the lush grass and the pasture ground.
Feel the tender pulsating heart of the Earth
that blesses you and every greenheart and balata tree,
the spotted Sandpiper, Scarlet Ibis, and Saki Winkie monkey.

Start by walking along the mudflats,
looking at the ungainly march of jumbie crabs.
And if they are still there for you to see,
pick ripened yellow "monkey" apples hidden on the tree.
Eat little wild jamuns until your tongue shows that coat of blue.
Dip your feet in the muddy waters.
How else will nature's defense comes to your aid
when the virus flies over barb-wired fences and locked gates?
Harden your body with a knowing of the wild,
and you will rise above others' flighty ways and guile.

Know the people around:
menders of shoes, those who lay stones, marble, and granite,
and those who lower their nets in the silent waters of the night.
Know those lumbering on sticks, drifters reeking of booze,
and those with tattoos of interlocking vines and dragons spitting fire.

And listen to stories of your ancestors
told by irrepressible chants and drums that resound
from Port Morant to Kamarang, Corentyne to Paramakatoi,
from the mines of Linden to the peaks of the Kanuku mountains.
Sway to the beat of the bongo, dolak, and tassa.
It still surges in the hearts of those who toiled hard
for you to reach the stars.

The Pink Lotus

I t's more than a sight to behold.
Its story—a timeless odyssey.

Born in the drowsiness of a slumber—
in the murky depths of the slimy pond,
but roused by a calling to gaze at the rising sun—
the pink lotus cuts the loathsome waters of the pond,
and opens its petals in the stillness of dawn.

A flower pure like the fire that rises from the ritual Havan.
When a mild wind stirs the silence,
the lotus dances with profuse blooms of celestial perfume.
.
At night it sinks into the depths of despair.
But a pilgrim's faith sheathed in this soul-inspired flower.
When night dies in day's soft embrace,
a quiet miracle on the pond displays.
In the awakening of meditative chants,
the pink lotus rises immaculately with blooms, defiant.

Kaieteur

K aieteur! Kaieteur! Kaieteur!
What words can tell of the unbridled power, and grandeur?
Torrents tumbling from the ledge of the Potaro River
to stern black rocks arresting their might in matted locks—
sending rainbows and clouds of mist over the rainforests,
and blessing them with a sublime freshness.

What festival of drums can drown the unrelenting thunder,
as the spirit of Makonaima roars over the vast Amazonia forest,
like ten thousand celestial horses galloping into a magical wilderness?

Cutting deep a gorge and rushing through the vast greenery.
A misty coolness to the carpet of purple orchids,
paying homage to a power, untrammeled and peerless

The eyes taken by this unearthly face;
finding what they have been searching these unnumbered days.
And if there's any unblemished Eden
where wildflowers and butterflies dance in the wind—
it's where Kaieteur makes that fearful yet playful plunge to Earth.

It's the Rainy Season

That great dome in vivid blue adorned,
and flourishes in white below
from the brush that painted
the flaming red on the robin's breast.

But between the span of a coffee break and a little talk,
that blaze of golden corn took leave of the land.
The air ceased to caress.
Curtains drawn on that splendid charm
hurriedly wrapped in blankets of grey,
and darker and darker with the stretch of day.

The low rumbling of far-off drums;
tiny rivulets dancing on windows,
and for all to know—
it's the rainy season
that brings gladness and urgency to every bloated drain,
and a swollen face to every trench, without the nagging pain.

The Mangroves

The mangroves—
    a tangled mess along the mudflats.
    The arching and interlocking of roots breathing in the open.
But in the confused commingling and closeness—
formidable garrisons stretched to tame the restless winds and tides
as the ocean's fever rises while we holler, bicker, and fight.

A ride on a kayak amidst serene mangroves along the river's bank.
A pristine canopy for crabs, jellyfish, sea anemones, and barnacles.
Where the cuckoo, snowy egret, and scarlet ibis
regale the wearied mind with songs,
and the searching rays of the sun warm every lonesome heart.

But what hardness of heart to displace the ancient mangroves?
Will it be the same coastland
when the mangroves are gone
and frenzied waves batter the strand?

This Blessed Land

This blessed land, where the fabled City of El Dorado born.
This lost world of pristine rainforests,
flora and fauna the world has yet to see.
Where the tabletop mountains of the Pakaraimas still proclaim
the silence that frightens the beast in humans.

You will be forgiven for thinking it's but a dream—
this land where love once roamed in unabashed nakedness,
and showed how to live as kith and kin
with all that dwell on earth, in the waters, and the air.
Where the daring spirit of the Amerindians live
in the Rupununi Savannahs and near the far-flung rivers.
Much to learn from their rituals, dances, and songs—
the people who know every healing herb, vine, and black caiman.

This blessed land where the winds greet coconut and saman trees,
smile at a vase of fresh flowers on the window sill,
and gently shakes the sash of the embroidered curtain.

No breaking news of the gathering strength of a storm,
and the urging to hunker down,
pile up layers of sandbags and board storefronts
to bear the force of a mad wild eye aiming at the shore,

This blessed land where mild wind and sweet rain send you to sleep,
and dream of orchids, misty air, and Kaieteur descending from Eden.
No howling winds lashing against trees and windows,
shaking the house, and people watching like sentinels of the night
as lightening and explosive bursts of transformers light up the sky,
and surging waters from the maddening rains and winds.

This blessed land where the door opens to the mild breeze.
There's no bitter biting air that cuts into the bones.
There's no frostbite from a short wait for a bus ride.
There's no blizzard when you cannot see your raised hand.
You wear simple cotton, but the wind plays with your hair.
You feel no pressing on the heart with thick, woolen layer on layer.

This blessed land where there's no rotating funnel-shaped cloud
moving over houses and buildings like a runaway freight train,
and leaving in its wake a war-torn landscape.
Where no dormant crater awakens with clouds of fire,
and molten lava rushing like a raging red river.

This blessed land where the Earth rests, but not in vexed silence.
She shows no temper; there are no violent tremors.
No chandelier oscillating on the ceiling,
no trophy or picture falling from the wall, and no floor moving.
No opening of the Earth that swallows roads, bridges, and towns.
There are no fault lines, except those we carry deep inside.

From Cuffy to Kowsilla

The taskmasters' whips dug roped tracks
   on their sun-burnt backs.
   The young bent with aged limbs;
tears mingled with disease-laden dust.
They cried for freedom.
Who would dare to raise a fist?

But Cuffy heard their cries;
their pains kept his anger alive.
He rose with an indomitable spirit.
He ignited the fire of the Berbice Slave Revolt.

That first shot heard far and wide.
It shook the planters' odious edifice.
It rallied others like Toussaint Louverture
to ride with the revolution's banner unfurled.
Freedom fighters resisted and defied
because Cuffy heard his brothers' cries.

In every land and clime we heard it sung in the day and night:
better to resist and die than cringe to evil's insolent might.
But for the sacrifices, raised voices, and protests of the brave,
we would not have lifted our eyes in that triumphant gaze
when the Golden Arrowhead in Atlantic's blithe wind was raised.

We remember the Enmore Martyrs:
Rambarran, Pooran, Lallabajee, Surajballi, and Harry.
Shot and killed in their prime; it was a vile crime.
And for what—to resist an unjust act:
to cut and load and break their backs on the slippery tracks.
But their names bestride this resplendent land,
and etched in glory undimmed by time and tide—

sung when folks gather at Enmore's sacred site.

And we remember Kowsilla,
and the brave women who stood shoulder to shoulder
on that fateful bridge at Leonora.
The depravity of the colonial masters,
and not the tractor, hewed down her body.
But her undying spirit unscathed,
and rises wherever people gather to resist blatant outrage.

And the mothers of this land can say one of their own
stood like intractable Roraima,
and saw in that misguided scab driver—
the loathsome eyes of the planters,
when Kowsilla's martyred blood hallowed the ground of Leonora.

Who Dares to Trample our Grass?

[Written when the Venezuelan government of Maduro made serious threats to Guyana's territorial integrity]

A loathsome itch, this unquenchable feverish thirst
to dare to trample our grass with heavy boots of steel,
and raise the dust that tells of a wretched incursion—
to erase the time-honored demarcation,
and grab—with a crooked line—the pristine Essequibo region.

A defiance in every current that rages through this land,
every wildflower, every blue saki and kiskadee, every jamun tree,
every vein of gold and diamond, and every grain of sand.
The leopard and cheetah will startle you with fire in their eyes
The black caiman will follow you at every step of every mile,
until you arrest this madness—this bellicose show—
to grow your far-flung legs, arms, and shoulders
by snatching a neighbor's mountains and rivers.

The jewel of Essequibo will never dazzle on your crown.
Let the silence along the Pakaraima mountains resound.
Stop this prattle; rest your drums and guns.
Your cup filled to the brim with the waters of the Orinoco;
you're choked with the black gold in its basin.
Why then this readiness to fight with a gentle neighbour
who relies on the watchful eyes of Mount Roraima,
and the stealthy steps of the prowling Jaguar?

The tributaries of the Essequibo River admonish your flawed map.
Not one feather of our toucan will fall on your lap,
nor will you take from a balata tree, one drop of blood or sap.

And if you spread your hairy hands over our savannahs and wetlands, the spirit of Makonaima will strike you with ten thousand fangs.

The Cricket Pitch

B efore, the crowd filled the stands.
Before the start of play—
I looked at the pitch; I studied every bit of it.

The pitch seemed all fine; it had not a patch of grass.
A little help for both ball and bat,
but not too much for one or the other to say:
"I knew it would crack before the end of match,"
"I knew it would be flat and a batter's paradise if ever there was."

But when the first ball went down the time-honored track,
we knew the pitch would decide the match.
It was a bag of tricks.
The ball flew off the bat and went straight to first or second slip.
It raised its head like a cobra; it spitted venom into the face.
It crept too low and crushed toes.
Every batter suffered some blows.

The ball screamed at bat and pad.
Every tentative push and every searching prod
found that outside edge or the rattle of death.
It swung, spun, and turned;
it came out from the fingers of a magician.
The crowd watched batter after batter—
a sad procession to the pavilion.

Uncle David got mad; he cursed the ground staff for a devilish pitch.
And like every batter, Uncle David got some good licks.

Another Bottle of Rum

He said with a smile but a sadness in his voice:
"I have found sweet forgetfulness in what's in my hand.
There's more than medicine in this bottle—
it's the very elixir that saves me from the ills of life.

I greet the day and sun with another bottle of rum,
and when I go to bed at night, the bottle I hold still tight.
No teacher, friend, or dear one has shown me the way;
the bottle calls out to me and like a believer, I obey."

Then I tapped him on the shoulder and said:
"Much of the world in some such state of drunkenness
though your much-lauded bottle we may not embrace.
Our robot-like motions muffle the awareness of the hummingbird,
keeping us too busy and stealing our hallowed days.

How little we hear the blue saki singing on treetops.
How little we watch wildflowers dancing beside the lake.
Would this double drunkenness
save us from the raging waters of the tempest?

Beware of forgetfulness—sleeping at high noon—
lest, before we know, the sands are through the neck of the hourglass.
Break the bottle and with it the illusion of a carefreeness.
Life: a most precious thing to lose, even for one priceless hour."

The Marketplace on a Saturday

They stare at you with colors of the rainbow.
They stare at you with scents and flourishes of the Earth.
They affirm what the seller shouts:
"Come! Come! Get you fresh bananas, oranges, mangoes,
eddoes, plantains, pineapples, and cassava."

The marketplace at Stabroek, Bourda, Buxton, Parika,
Corentyne, Skeldon, Mahaica, Kurupukari, and Bartica.
They tell of the richness of farms, ocean, and creeks.
It's bustling, haggling, shouting, cajoling and the comingling of faces,
music and laughter and assorted things not in other places.

Look at saigans, cashews, sapodillas, ginips and arawas—
huddled in heaps raised to exaggerate their smiles.
And if you doubt the freshness of the take from backdam,
mudflats and swamp—watch hassas jumping out of quake,
crabs crawling out of barrel, and shrimps leaping for nearest drain.

It's the marketplace where you knock at a whole pumpkin,
and if the sound rings not true, you choose a slice or two.
It's where you place a string of patwas or houris on shoulder,
stuff your basket with gingerbread, salara, and bottles of cassareep,
and buy an iguana and the liver and kidneys of a goat or sheep.

Not all smiles when the price of a miserly bundle of bora
sends a chill and fever on a sun-drenched Saturday morning.
When prices sit at giddy heights, mothers stare at lukanani, kurass,
gilbaka, and basha, and a handful of hot, hot wiri-wiri
peppers for pepperpot, cookup, metemgee, and duck curry.

But the crowds come.
The laughter, shouting, and the beating of drums,

stalls stretched for miles; a festival along the roadside.
Who would dare to miss the marketplace on a Saturday?

Crossing the Demerara River

The captain brought the ferry close to the landing.
Timbers cringed at the blows to their barnacles-infested joints.
The burly man threw out the fat ropes;
the MV Makouria moored at the Vreed-en-Hoop Stelling.

School children jostled for a seat on the ferry.
I watched choppy waters, and the city jutting out from misty clouds.
I saw the ship that was always there: the Saguenay.

There were familiar sights on the ferry:
the blind man whose pleas melted the stone-hearted,
and the pretty girl who sold salted nuts from a basket.

Lovers held hands and basked in the wind-swept mist.
A fight or two when men argued and lost their wits.
A preacher spoke of the end and admonished all to repent.

But before the story told or a card game or two,
the gangway dropped, and people pushed and shoved
for a glance at the "Big Market" Stabroek clock.

And when the day at school, office, factory, or shopping done,
folks headed for the ferry on a sun-drenched afternoon,
and for the daunting fun of crossing the Demerara River.

Mattie told Mattie

We listened to the oversized radio on the wall,
or the little transistor we placed near a bowl of hot dahl.
It's how we got the breaking news of the day.
We shouted it from window to window and over the fence.

But the real story came from the street corner or near the barber's tent.
Mattie told mattie what the air waves never did carry.
We added flair and color, layer upon layer, and more twists
to every news than in those magic ribbons dancing under the mandap.

Mattie told mattie when someone died in the village.
Then we knew the fortune left behind.
One who never drank one drop of rich red wine,
or ever lowered hands in giving,
but first in line on every news of a taking

Mattie told mattie when a child was born in the village.
Then we knew the father was a magician
who defied deadbolt locks and windows grilled with iron.
Loretta, the parrot, saw it all and riled at the father who celebrated,
though not one of his features stamped on sweet infant's face.

Mattie told mattie of every wedding in the village.
Then we knew big Bertie had no choice
but to marry for a wrong turn late into the night.
And what fate brought to gentle Bertie for a sudden change of mind.

Part Two

Reflections along the Way

A Precious Little Time

You blow out the flickering candles.
You sing the jolly tune.
You are too young to ask where the years have gone.

But the Peregrine Falcon has not, out of spite,
taken your fun-filled years in its lordly flight.
If you were to live these impressionable years again,
there would still be some cause to complain;
to curse a bending lane or two:
"If only this could have happened"—
the most useless, despairing words spoken or written.

Grab the years to court, dance, and know and mend your ways.
When the lifespan of a distant star is too short—
a precious little time is all you have.
What good does it bring to waste the hours
with thoughts of what might have been?
Make the hours count; give them wings to fly
with a smile, a helping hand,
and a heart seeking to understand.

A Word of Cheer

A word of cheer to a friend or passerby—
count it as a thing of value,
though not as enduring as a planted tree
or a well dug in a far-flung country.

We may never know the measure of its worth;
it's bound for the credit side in the ledger book of life.
And if the word is never said,
but you send to another a thought of kindness:
that sweet impulse brings a brightness on your face
like when you raise your hand to erase a wrong.

How little we know of the battle raging in another's mind
more vexing by the icy winds of our unfeelingness.
But a word of cheer—a balm that heals
wounds not revealed in harrowing incisions on the skin,
but deep within the psyche of a human being.

Oh, Little Stream

Oh, little stream with a gentle spirited rhythm.
A mean rock mocks your rousing movement.
It looks you in the face and blocks your way.
Don't just lament; don't just stay.
Don't wait for someone to build you a stairway.

You have the blue saki and moco-moco bush to greet,
and the parched lips of the para grass to soothe.
Step aside the stingy rock and move along.
The world will reckon you wise and strong.

You need to know it's not all groovy and smooth.
There's work to do—undergrowth to bend your way through.
Don't just stare at the vines choking the cherry tree.
You need to know the world's a little less kind.
Look to none to find your way on a day dark and dreary

A Hard Life

H is was a hard life,
as much from the fell clutch of circumstances
as from the reverberated sounds he sent forth.
A roughness he knew,
more poignant when he sang of a lost love,
and the meanness of a world that fed his bitterness.

He looked older than his years,
though not one to be burdened with cares.
He knew little of his strength—it was that of a bull,
and what ill-use with fights, wounds, and booze.

He cut the canes in the blazing sun.
He laid the nets in the distant, silent waters of the night.
He tamed every bad dog, rode every wild horse,
and tumbled wheelbarrows of sand and bricks.
And still a spark of finesse in those harrowed hands
when he played sweet music on the face of the steelpan.

Roots

The snake-like roots of the mango tree
buckle and make a sham of the slick concrete.
Entrenched around jagged rocks in the silence of the Earth,
they seek the vigor of the depths that spills upwards.

What but the roots to boast of eyes that thrive with no sleep or rest
and see beyond the dug darkness?
There, they probe and plow and hold fast to a veiled bastion—
a sprawling network that makes the clouds wonder what power
holds the tree to look over high tension wires and the mighty river,
like a lighthouse that watches over the dark, deep waters.

The tree at that dizzy height
stretches far and wide to show its might.
But the roots farrow deeper for a stronghold,
lest the stalwart tree in its pride dares to mock the raging tide.

And we not tethered to the Earth,
need to know our roots and wrap our hearts around
with songs, dances, and festive drums.
For in youth and age, the roots open the gates of life.
And in the ill winds of a storm, the roots are strong and steady
like a fortress overlooking the city and anchors in the deep blue sea.

The River Waits

T he river waits, waits, and waits.
It's the call of an effusive heart
that knows no rest even when the hours grow dark,

The river waits, waits, and waits.
Heed the primordial call of the waves.
They long to embrace your feet stripped of woolen care.

The river waits, waits, and waits.
Shake off this faint-heartedness—
this aloofness that guards the feet from getting wet.

The river waits, waits, and waits.
Why are you afraid of the murkiness and uneven depths?
It's but an illusion—this concrete upholstered evenness.

The river waits, waits, and waits.
Go, go into the river with bold steps.
Feel the pull of current and sound the depths.

The river waits, waits, and waits
See its expansiveness, the shoreline still receding,
and how far you have veered from where you started.

The Old Man Planted a Tree

The old man planted a tree along the dusty pathway.
He watched it grow day by day.
In the night when the wind howled and mauled the sapling,
he felt the aching; he sent it a blessing
and waited for the morning to see
the tender tree blushing and smiling.
He broke into a song when he saw a spreading of its arms.
But the old man died before the tree grew tall and strong.

He never took a little rest under its inviting shade.
He never saw on its branch the nest the robin made
or on its leaf the Monarch butterfly in a stealthy sleep.
He never knew how it braved the storms and lightning
and kept standing in the scorching sun and fearsome wind.

But the old man understood these things all along—
he would never see the tree stretching its arms
to every trembling blue saki or kiskadee,
and steadying its feet in a climbing that makes the cowherd boy giddy.

And that's why he planted it with a smile and a song—
for you and me and the world to see,
the beauty of life that's in a tree.

To Set a Mind Ablaze

The crowded classroom—
never the same as the woods, fields, hills, and pasture ground
calling you to play, sing, and dance in rain, wind, and sun.
sink your feet in soft mud,
and test the depth of the pond where little fishes abound.

Cramped in an aisle of monotony;
regimented and drilled,
and the mind like a bucket to fill—
never the same as to set a mind ablaze;
to behold the shimmering gold the sun made for the sea's tranquil face.

In time, you will know how this distraught world
longs to gaze at the rising sun and gulls circling in flight,
hear waves lapping the shoreline, and feel the morning
rush of the wind, but with your eyes and ears
and a heart quivering with untouched strings.

A Smile and a Song

Open the windows at dawn
with a smile and a song.
Greet the rising sun and the world.
Take in the scent of the chameli and jasmine.
Gaze at the circled flights of robins.
The gladness to live and hear and see,
and you will hasten the day along
and reveal a heart that belongs to nature
that smiles and sings day long.

Two lovers meet beside a pond.
A smile greets a song.
They kiss and hold hands,
and no place for what ails the world
in their eager, tight embrace.

The power in a smile and a song—
the storms they have becalmed.
It's worth all the miles you walk
to befriend one who smiles
at the bending path further,
and hums a song with love's fervor.

Waylaid along this Beaten Way

Little candles flickering on the ice cream cake.
But to have never lived even for one day,
as if waylaid along this beaten way
where it's all about making a living.

Too much hustling, shoving, and grabbing—
too little knowing, feeling, and caring.
Too much talking and bickering—
too little loving and inward-looking.

To be estranged from the music of the spheres,
and suffer the mind to bear a thousand cares.
To think it's all about that clever talk and guile,
and forget what it means to roam in the wild,
watch the sun rising, the tides rushing in glee,
and regale the heart with songs of the robin and the kiskadee.

An Affirmation

To be cynical about love is to be a stranger to life.
In an embrace and a kiss are life's secrets revealed
and not in the mortification of the flesh—
the denial of life's bliss.
Shorn of love, it's a world of vacant stares and no music in the air.
It's a balm that gives a spring to our steps and makes the heart mellow.

Look for the star in the beloved's eyes
before you hunt it down from the unbounded sky.
It's a razor's edge you walk when your mind recoils
from what keeps the robins and sparrows singing into the dark.

When love beckons, walk as if in a temple.
It's the winged chariot that leaves behind vexations of the spirit.
And to be in a warm bed in the beloved's arms—
not a forgetfulness of a world in the icy winds of unfeelingness,
but an affirmation of what the Universe declares in celestial songs.

This is Your Day

This is your day.
  Cram its hours with music and songs,
  thoughts and words no less fruitful
than labor that furrowed the fields,
and hands lifted with bread
for those who intimately know the pangs of neglect.

This is your day.
Grab it to mend fences along the way,
befriend a fellow traveler, a wildflower,
share cherished memories and laughter.
Stamp on this day the things engraved in your heart.
Watch how robins on the treetops dart.

This is your day.
Treat it not like an intruder at your gate.
This day has long waited for you.
Embrace it as your friend, too.
Lose it not in self-pity, in regret.
Unfurl the sails for adventures ahead.

This is your day.
With nothing to do, it's still fair use of the day.
But be aware of the hour and the season.
The butterflies and the gulls know them well,
and if you happen to rest in a hammock by the shore,
listen to the eternal music of the sea.

A Thousand Suns Blazing for You

When the world comes with rude bumps and shocks—
baffling and not comforting like the classroom—
I wish I could shield you from the ill winds, scorching sun,
and wild beasts prowling around.

Those who hold you close know what it means when the world's
encroaching to steal your smiles and clip your wings.
What it means to fall and take the bruises,
but not like the bruises of your childhood days.
There are no marks and no blood stains from wounds deep within.

That's when you need to roam along hills and hear the love birds sing,
lest a loneliness creeps into your being and steals your days and nights.
A gruesome thing that would silence the drums, cymbals, and guitar,
leave dust to gather in your room, cobwebs to dangle from the ceiling,
and that would feign a smile to see you crawl another mile.

But even as you walk with a fearful beat along the rugged trails
and thoroughfares where the music blares—
if you could only know—hands are reaching to you:
a thousand suns blazing for you.

On the Wings of a Silence

L isten to that meditative stillness.
Waves caressing the shore; brooks gurgling in the woods.
Humble bizi-bizi and moco-moco bush swaying in the breeze.
Tiny birds, butterflies, bees, frogs, and insects in an animated fanfare
that brings the wearied mind to cheer,
and the commingling of a multitude of sounds, soft and alluring,
but foreign to ears that bleed from discordant drums—

and you know it must be the night fast approaching
on the wings of a silence that drowns the vexations of the day.
A respite from the staccato and vroom vroom of cars and motorbikes,
and the brutal blaring noise from the distorted faces of boom boxes
that gives a thumping to the beleaguered nerves and heart.

Rejoice in the plentitude of such soothing, quiescent sounds.
A time may come when they're no longer around.
And what a poverty in that prosperity—
clouds leaving a glum trail over thoroughfares and high rises—
when we hear no bees buzzing on the silk cotton tree,
and no frogs croaking in swollen ponds by the deserted churchyard.

A Felt Closeness

Not from that little smart ubiquitous thing
that knows no rest and brings the whole world
into the the living room or the conference—
but people talking to people in a felt closeness of a tap
on the shoulder, a look into the eyes, and a warm embrace.

Something lost when a distance intervenes.
We talk by holding or looking at a screen.
A lonesomeness creeps in when we talk and talk,
but there's no fence to lean on,
no long bench on the cow dung-smeared ground on which to sit
and feel each other's pulse as the narrative shifts.

The leaves talk in such closeness on a bending limb.
Roses huddled on a tree;
they sing and dance like in a merry band.
The birds converse in their circled flights,
but no cloud barges between their flapping wings.

The touch of a warm hand—
more than words can ever say,
or smiles at the other end apprehend.
Walking side by side in the balmy air;
every newcomer—another embrace,
another warm face to behold,
and heart-to-heart, soul to soul
along the beaten ways of the world.

This Interconnectedness

The loud brum, brum, brum of chainsaws in the rainforest.
No blood dripping from dogged, cruel jaws.
No agonizing cries of a brutal death heard.

But the forests, rivers, and mountains grieve for the felled tree.
They know it's more than the loss of a tree to the vast greenery.
They know the hands that wield the blade will not cease to itch
until swathes of the lush rainforest razed, tree by tree.

What will the clouds do that kiss the forest with a love so tender?
And the tapir, puma, and bushmaster when they have no trees to greet?
What fate holds for the Sackie Winkie monkeys and baboons
as they gazed with startled eyes at this sacrilege to the rainforest?

Where will the abounding insects, bees, birds, and butterflies rest?
They give to the wilderness the sounds of music at no one's behest.
And what's this callousness for the way of life of the indigenous tribes
for whom the forest is as sacred as the feathers that adorn their head?

And we who think little of the worth of the rainforest,
will come to feel this interconnectedness—
this circle of life with magic in every bird that glides with the wind,
and every leaf that breathes with a stirring speech—
when the tides rush in every town and village to reclaim the streets,
and we jump into every trench for relief from the unrelenting heat.

A Gaff

We knew Riley was a real gaff man when he told the boys
how he wrestled a jumbie at the backdam.

We love to gaff and gaff and gaff—
an art, our very own, like clapping paratha roti,
like savoring, in the purine leaf, the 'seven curry.'

You say it's just talk and talk,
but there's much more to a gaff.
It springs from that uncommon ground to startle
and shock and make us to believe the most outlandish things.
And if you think you have heard it all before,
then you have never heard a gaff from a tailor rethreading the needle,
or a from a carpenter laying the tiles along the floor.

And if the world wants to know who we are as a people,
then take not our pulse, or reckon our faults,
but listen to our gaff at the bottom house,
at the street corner or the neighborhood shop.
It's bound to bring a respite to all this sordid talk,
this crass and graft, and spite in this blighted world,
and regale the heart with what it wants to hear.

What if every day is sun-drenched—
it's still dreary if we hear no gaff.

Naked in the Wind

Marvel at the little butterflies.
Look at the dance of sun-drenched orchids and wildflowers.
They ask for nothing but a little of your time.
To step back for a while,
unencumbered of the trappings and wearisome noise,
and know the silence the world ever so denies.

They wouldn't have you raising your hands
and clenching your fists to declare a creed.
They wouldn't make you to dread for having a doubt, a disbelief.
They know you're still a child seeking relief from the sun's eye.
They wouldn't abandon you when you have nothing to give or show,
save for being naked in the wind seeking to be free.

If only the world could show such broad-mindedness
as the little butterflies, wildflowers, and sun-drenched orchids.

One Sprightly Dance

A wildflower dancing in the wind,
a gentle surf along the shore, the allure of the cliffs—
unerringly divine what they give to the heart and mind,
but without the tinseled wrappings on gifts;
without ornaments strung on poetic lines.

There's something far greater than the finest of our arts,
more akin to the wonder arising deep within,
in what Nature sends straight to the human heart.

When Nature writes or makes an utterance—
no need to interpret the cadence of the language and music.
And a million verses on dusty pages couldn't tell half as much
as what a wildflower does in one sprightly dance.

What the World Teaches You

The world teaches you how to make a living—
hustling, outdoing, making a name and a fortune.
How to speak with a smooth and clever tongue
and cover cracks in walls all around.
How to march with strident steps
and raise your hands to declare a creed and a belief.
To fall in line, stick with the clan,
and remember the drill, though you will never be part of a battle plan.

But how to endure the fury of the waves that beat upon your shore,
to know that feeling that impels all things into being,
and how to play your part in a drama of ever-changing scenes—
not one lesson.
Not one line drawn along the sands of time
to discern the pristine from the blighted grime.

And when you stand along the sun-kissed strand
reckoning all you have learned,
you will find something missing—
how to open your wings to the inviting wind.

The world teaches you to be too clever,
like a blade too sharp in the hands of a careless child.
But has it ever taught you how to think and just be,
to sip a cup of country lemonade under the coconut tree,
to roam with the falcon, blazing across the sky,
and see into the heart of all things, unsightly or bright.

The world teaches you to outshine.
What an applause when you're the first to cross the finish line.
But who will tap you on the shoulder
for cradling a little trembling robin in your palms

or listening to the sad, sad story of a homeless man?

Along the Shore

Take a stroll along the shore.
There's time here to think,
and listen to the pounding of the surf.

Take a slow, deep measure of fresh air,
and give back every bit,
but charged with your fears.
It's a thin, fragile golden thread,
but priceless—all things on it rest—
this incoming and outgoing of the breath.

It's not the place for a dashing hat,
and gaudiness that suffocates the gladness.
The wind likes to play on your hair and skin.
There's little rhythm on felt, worsted wool, and silk.
The sea does not like to see a sour face.
Smile with every fisherman who brings in the haul,
and when you hear the seagulls' call.

When sun beats down on sea and sand,
listen to sweet calypso and steelpan.
The closest thing to your Eden—
to drink a cup of country lemonade
in a hammock under the shade of coconut palms.

When musicians, steelpan players, and revelers gone
and none but you, the waves and rocks, and a gliding falcon—
in that breathtaking silence,
listen to the timeless symphony of the sea.

You will hear a message unerringly divine
that needs no applause from human hands.

You will enter a temple,
but there will be no utterance from any priest.

A Treasured Thing

Hold the book; open it.
Run your fingers along its spine.
Turn the pages and feel them.

Take in that whiff of fresh ink on crisp paper.
It's the best perfume.
It will enter your soul and be there when you're old.

A good book—a treasured thing.
But don't have it buried with dust and grime
like faded newspapers stacked away.

Keep your eyes on it—it's tempting even for the wise.
Hold it close to your heart,
and feel the thrill of its magic and mystery.

Loss of that charm when it's hidden in that overcrowded screen.
It's warm in your hands—you want to read, read, and read.
You watch words leaping off the page faster than a screaming jet,
but still there when you close the book for a little rest.
You are in a coral isle, a dense forest of indigenous tribes,
but you board no plane, bus, or train, cross no river or sea,
show no ticket or luggage, or even unlock your gate.

You will know of adventures and exploits,
courage and heroism, and characters colorful and weird.
But not like listening to the tales of an old rover of the seas.
You will be there in the heat of every action.
You will wield the blade; you will hold the poison-dart frog,
and wonder as Kaieteur descends from Eden to a carpet of orchids.

Drawings on the Sidewalk

See the the gladness on the face of the sidewalk
when decorated with fat-colored chalks.
Look at the stars, yet unnamed.
The flowers opening their petals in the gentle rain.
Behold the templates of childhood joy, and fun-filled games—
all on the sidewalk—what little hands can do in the jubilant air.

Then I think of the children in war-torn lands.
When they gather the scattered crayons to draw or make a mark,
we see no splendid flowers, no rolling hills,
and no gull cutting the air over the tranquil sea.
Their hands draw seared images of carnage
on what remains of their blood-stained sidewalk.

Machines bristling with frightening power.
A carnival of death coming nearer and nearer.
A payload of explosive fire and thunder;
sirens screaming, mothers wailing and beating their chests.
Children buried under pillars and slabs of concrete;
little hands in the rubble clutching a doll and a biscuit.

The sun no longer looks but hides its face
when earth and sky ablaze, and not from a brilliance,
but a ghoulish dance that's ever our disgrace.

Such Sleep

The cat curls up on a bed of yellow leaves
along a beaten fence near a bending mango tree.
Its blanket is the blithe Atlantic breeze;
its pillows are the rocks beneath the fallen leaves.

No one sings a lullaby to send it to sleep.
Yet, see how sound and still it sleeps,
like the dew that settles on the tip of a leaf,
like the quiet of the churchyard in the midday heat.

If we could know even a paltry measure of such sleep,
how less harrowed and weary our days would be.
We little rest on our silken beds, our pillows of warm velvet,
but endless twists and turns, as if bristled with thorns,
and miles and miles and miles, the mind burns
before a little sleep touches down.

There's something unearthly in how the cat sleeps.
A star watches from the boundless deep.
In its track of matchless glory—
it loves to snatch a stretch of such sleep.

Noise! Noise! Noise!

It violates the silence of the sacred space—
damning as invading the temple or any other sacrilege.
It offends the trees, but they cannot leave for Mainstay Lake.
They protest but constrained to stay.
The puppies, kittens, sheep, and chickens bewail their fate
that they dwell among those who need to amplify
every whisper, every secret, and every dream to tell.

It's noise, noise, and noise everywhere.
Senseless that delight when others need to forbear,
and wish they could be impervious to every box that blares
in a van or car, on a cart along the thoroughfare, or the stairs.

Unwind to wipe that frown from your face.
When strobing lights stalk the night, and the DJ incites the party,
gyrate on the floor like a multi-colored spinning top
and shake those buttocks and hips like reeds in the wind.
But think of the injury to the ears when the music blares
that you cannot hear your friend even when she swears.

The old and the sick pleaded for a rest,
when the music raised to the decibel of a screaming jet.
And what respite when the music turned off—
the staccato of motorbikes, wailing sirens, and jackhammers pounding
before the windows early in the morning.

Will the Amazonica Lily hear screeching brum-brum of chainsaws?
Will armadillos and jaguars lament the invasion of their ground?
Will noise, noise, and noise blanket the land end to end?
It's already entrenched when every talking is shouting.

The Crowd

Be in the crowd,
but know it can be a beastly thing
that with one mind thinks,
and crushes the Monarch butterfly's wings.
So often sanity stumbles in the surging crowd,
and then the bricks, chairs, and bottles,
burnt stores, cars and tires, Molotov cocktails,
exploding canisters of tear gases and cannon balls of water.

The crowd no love song sings.
You hear no sound of a pure gushing spring.
But one hoarse, riotous voice
and blaring, frightful drums.
See the dust and debris blinding.
See every bird fleeing,
and leaves of every tree trembling,
as if from a fearful wind.

But, if not for the surging crowd at the city's gates,
many an insolent, bloated principality would remain unscathed.
When there are cries for bread, and it's time to redress a wrong—
compelling are the throbbing drums of the crowd.

Clouds

Sometimes, like cotton balls clustered under the deep blue sky.
Sometimes like fluffy mountains lazily floating—
stretched by an invisible hand into familiar and weird forms:
a dragon spitting fire
a soldier in battle armor
a preacher inspired
an island in the Essequibo River
a template of erotic desire—
and those gently sailing high
like feathers of the ostrich kissing the sky.

Rushing for an unpremeditated gathering.
Looking down on the pasture ground,
hearing the thunder of battle drums,
and seeing blinding white tributaries in the sky—
heeding the call to die with dark, portentous looks
sending streams of arrows on tents and roofs,
fields of cane and rice, and backs of deer and capybaras.

A Moment in Time

I t's all we have; it's all we can call our own.
But it's more than enough,
and what a gift to see a child, a pebble, a flower,
and the time-honored river as we never did before.

A moment in time.
It's ever born; it's never really born.
Wrapped in it, all worlds and galaxies whirling,
and all the suns blazing.
But who will gaze at a vision so blinding?
Who can see at once all the waves of all the oceans rolling?
But between their coming and going,
it's a moment in time still proclaiming,
whether we hear it, or shout it down in disdain,
or our wonted illusion thinks it's all the same.

A moment in time.
When the wind rushes and makes sketches upon the sand.
When a bird flees its tattered cage,
and the curtain opens on the stage.

A moment in time.
When the first raindrop kisses the pond,
a canary bursts into a song,
and the peacock opens its iridescent fan.

A moment in time.
When the winner of a marathon crosses the finish line,
and an infant announces its arrival,
not with smiles but cries.

A moment in time.
When a star in a distant galaxy is born,
and another shredded into ribbons.

Heatwave

It's not the same sun as in my childhood days.
Then it warmed the heart and made strong our sinews and bones.
It healed bruises on the knee and watched with glee our play
on the pasture ground, till we couldn't see the ball around.
We never ran from the sun; we waited and waited
for the red-breasted robin to alight on the gum-coated tree.
But what have we done to provoke the sun?

Days when the fire in its eyes scorching the ground,
burning forests, melting roads and bridges, blasting towns.
Where's that shield, pristine through the ages,
to guard against this seething wave of torment
sapping the vitals of humans and beasts as we implore
the heavens to open the gates with a flood of relief?

People throwing bottled water on faces,
jumping into the ocean, rivers, lakes, and trenches.
Who would not delight in a splash when the air, a boiling cauldron?
Who would object when some bare it all;
when every undergarment feeds fire on skin?

What dreaded fires will stalk the land in a hundred years?
Will we ever learn; will we mend our ways?
Will we see the face that warmed my childhood days?

A Passing Shower

Dense dark clouds overhanging;
a low rolling of distant drums,
but not from the waves breaking along the shoreline.
There, all calm save for the ocean's celestial song.

It's a passing shower lifting downcast faces of sunflowers,
awakening drains, ditches, trenches, rivers,
crabs, butterflies, and hosts of insects.
Uprush of a refreshing breeze,
and scent of fresh earth, twigs, and leaves.

Then, as if by magic weaved,
the sun again,
as if it never rained.

And when it's all over—
the red breasted robin shaking off droplets of water.

Sail On, Sail On

There's a ship out there.
She rides the sea with ease.
The waves climb to break her bones.
She shows a steady bow and stern.
She bestrides the danger with composure.
An unyielding power in her keel—
such nerves of steel.

A rare defiance to a sea angry, restless, and turbulent.
No blast from wind or wave;
no surging current in the dark depths
to dampen her spirit and delay her course set.

On the sea of life straddled before our eyes
like that ship we should ride.
There will be storms and currents swift and surging.
Unnumbered things may go wrong,
but we need to sail on,
but we need to sail on.

To Write and Erase

I am a child who has just begun to write and erase.
Someone guides my unsteady fingers as I trace the orbit of a star.

I have yet to learn the ways of the world.
I have yet to learn the ways of humans:
the cares and fires in their heart,
how they betray the things they say,
and turn every bright red ribbon into shades of gray.

What freshness in these dogmas, rituals, and beliefs?
What charm in these narratives of unfeelingness
standing like unending columns of mist that would not lift,
barring the sky, the sun's eye, and a falcon gliding over the cliffs?

Is it not enough that I know these rolling hills and fields,
dew-laden grass, gushing streams, every wildflower,
and every kiskadee that breaks the stillness with a song?
They give a contentment that feeds the hours.
The closest I may ever come to feeling that uninhibited bliss
that eludes the heart and mind as soon as we begin to speak of it.

There will always be a child who has just begun to write and erase.

About the Author

Haimnauth Ramkirath was born in the Republic of Guyana, perched at the very tip of South America. He grew up in a small village of rustic beauty and charm, where the rhythms of life were simple and predictable. As a child, he immersed himself completely in the fascination and beauty of the natural world. This love for nature is still one of the abiding joys of his life, and is reflected in many of his poems.

Haimnauth was a teacher for almost ten years at the secondary school level in Guyana. He came to the USA in 1991. He is a professional Accountant who has worked his way up to the Controller level. He lives in Bayonne, NJ with his wife, Radhika, his daughter, Tamala, and son, Akash. Haimnauth is an ardent practitioner of Meditation and Yoga.

Haimnauth has published five works of poetry: *At Ease Like the Blooming Lotus, Troubled World, Rhythms of Ease & Wonder, Unsung Verses*, and *Stirrings of Hope & Other Poems*. This is his sixth work.

9 781736 373347